GEORGE
AND
MARTHA

For George and Cecille

The stories in this book were originally published by Houghton Mifflin
Company in *George and Martha*.
Copyright © 1972 by James Marshall
Copyright © renewed 2000 by Sheldon Fogelman

www.hmhbooks.com

First Green Light Readers edition 2010

The Library of Congress Cataloging-in-Publication Data is on file.
ISBN: 978-0-618-96331-7 hardcover
ISBN: 978-0-547-40624-4 paperback

Manufactured in China
LEO 10 9 8 7 6 5 4 3 2
4500273383

George and Martha

written and illustrated by
JAMES MARSHALL

sandpiper

Green Light Readers
HOUGHTON MIFFLIN HARCOURT
BOSTON   NEW YORK

TWO STORIES ABOUT TWO GREAT FRIENDS

STORY NUMBER ONE

SPLIT PEA SOUP

Martha was very fond of making split
pea soup. Sometimes she made it
all day long. Pots and pots of split
pea soup.

If there was one thing that George was not fond of, it was split pea soup. As a matter of fact, George hated split pea soup more than anything else in the world. But it was so hard to tell Martha.

One day after George had eaten ten
bowls of Martha's soup, he said to
himself, "I just can't stand another
bowl. Not even another spoonful."
So, while Martha was out in the
kitchen, George carefully poured the
rest of his soup into his loafers under
the table.
"Now she will think I have eaten it."
But Martha was watching from
the kitchen.

"How do you expect to walk home with your loafers full of split pea soup?" she asked George.

"Oh dear," said George. "You saw me."

"And why didn't you tell me that you hate my split pea soup?"

"I didn't want to hurt your feelings," said George.

"That's silly," said Martha. "Friends should always tell each other the truth. As a matter of fact, I don't like split pea soup very much myself. I only like to make it. From now on, you'll never have to eat that awful soup again."

"What a relief!" George sighed.

12

"Would you like some chocolate
chip cookies instead?" asked Martha.
"Oh, that would be lovely," said George.
"Then you shall have them," said
his friend.

STORY NUMBER TWO

The Flying Machine

"I'm going to be the first of my
species to fly!" said George.
"Then why aren't you flying?"
asked Martha. "It seems to me that you
are still on the ground."
"You are right," said George. "I don't
seem to be going anywhere at all."
"Maybe the basket is too heavy,"
said Martha.

"Yes," said George, "I think you are right again. Maybe if I climb out, the basket will be lighter."

"Oh dear!" cried George. "Now what have I done? There goes my flying machine!"

"That's all right," said Martha. "I would rather have you down here with me."

Crossword Puzzle

Use clues from "Split Pea Soup" and "The Flying Machine" to complete the puzzle! Answers at the bottom of the page.

Across

1. Kind of chips in Martha's cookies.
2. What no hippo has done before.
3. Number of bowls of split pea soup George ate.
4. Where George's flying machine ended up.

Down

1. Room where Martha makes her soup.
2. Where George poured his soup.
3. The problem with George's basket.

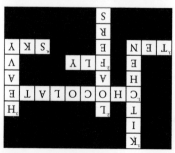

Fill in the blank. Answers at the bottom of the page.

1. Martha was very _____*good*_____ of

   making split pea soup.

2. George _____*don't like*_____ split pea soup more

   than anything else in the world.

3. George didn't want to hurt Martha's

   _____*feeling*_____.

4. George was going to be the _____*first*_____

   of his species to fly.

5. Martha would _____*like*_____ have George

   on the ground with her.

More fun activities to do at home!

Draw a picture of yourself.

Draw a picture of your best friend.

Make a list of foods you are fond of.

Make a list of foods you hate.

Draw a picture of your very favorite food!